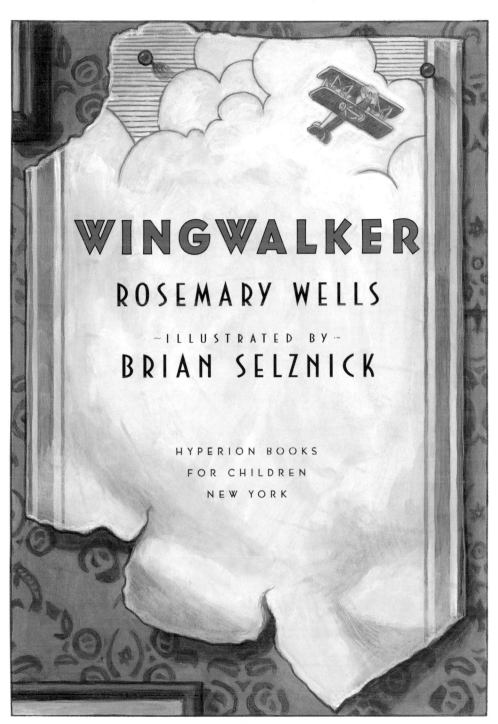

WINGWALKER

ROSEMARY WELLS

~ILLUSTRATED BY~

BRIAN SELZNICK

HYPERION BOOKS
FOR CHILDREN
NEW YORK

CONNOLLY

Printed in Singapore
FIRST EDITION
1 3 5 7 9 10 8 6 4 2
The illustrations in this book were done with acrylic paints on unprimed watercolor paper.

Library of Congress Cataloging-in-Publication Data
Wells, Rosemary.
Wingwalker / Rosemary Wells; illustrated by Brian Selznick.— 1st. ed.
p.   cm.
Summary: During the Depression, Reuben and his out-of-work parents move from Oklahoma to
Minnesota, where his father gets a job as a carnival wingwalker and Reuben has a chance to
overcome his terror of flying.
ISBN 0-7868-0397-5 (hc) — ISBN 0-7868-2347-X (lib)
[1. Fairs—Fiction. 2. Stunt flying—Fiction. 3. Fear—Fiction. 4. Depressions—1929—
Fiction. 5. Fathers and sons—Fiction. 6. Minnesota—Fiction.] I. Selznick, Brian, ill. II. Title.
PZ7.W46843 Wi 2002
[Fic]—dc21
2001039087

For Lisa
—R.W.

For Noel Silverman,
who has been there from the start
—B.S.

CHAPTER ONE

SMALL WORLD

I LIKED TO LOOK OUT at the world from our attic window. The land that circled Ambler, Oklahoma, was silky green prairie. Here and there you could spot an oil drilling station with a drilling rig pumping away like a big iron grasshopper.

I believed that I could see the whole world from that attic window. I believed that nothing in it would ever change but the seasons of the year; that no one ever died except very old people whom I did not know. I was just beginning the second grade.

On the edge of town was a piece of highway, abandoned as soon as it had been started. You had to cross the railroad tracks into the cornfields to find it. My father said he could spit from one end to the other of it. All the same, it made a landing strip. That's where they held the 1933 Oklahoma Air Races.

My father was a barrel-shaped man with small shiny feet in Ever-Glo Quality shoes. He liked nothing in the whole world more than airplanes. Father took me and my cousin, Mary Ellen Hockerbee, out to see them race.

We sat in the highest row of the traveling grandstand. Father said we had the best seats, considering everybody looked at the sky. In my pocket was my ticket.

"The winning ticket is number eight

twenty-nine!" announced the loudspeaker. "The lucky winner gets a ride in the passenger seat of our Oklahoma Champion. Stand by, everybody!"

"Didn't win!" said Mary Ellen. She shredded her ticket and it floated to the ground many sections below our feet. "I never win anything!" she added in her squeaky-door voice.

My father knew that voice. He promised Mary Ellen an all-day sucker to keep her from pouting.

I held my breath and curled my ticket. It slid from my fingers to the safety of the ticket blizzard in the grass below.

Mary Ellen's eyes followed me like a horsefly. If she found out I had chickened out of my winning airplane ride, Mary Ellen would tell the whole school before anyone so much as pledged allegiance Monday morning.

She grabbed my ticket from the bench below us where it landed, and waved it around for the world to see.

"Number eight twenty-nine! You won, scaredy-cat!" Mary Ellen pointed out each of the three numbers. "Girly-pants mama's boy!" she sang. "I'm telling the whole class you have little tiny rosebuds on your underpants and you're a 'fraidy cat of the airplane."

"Take my ticket, Father! Take it!" I whispered. I squinted into the smile on my father's face. I tried to will him to see how my heart was quivering right there in my mouth like a lump of Jell-O. Father guessed nothing. He would have given his right arm for a ride in that plane.

"Reuben isn't afraid of a thing on earth, Mary Ellen," he told her. I saw pride shining in his eyes like stars. If I did not go, I would forever cut a little diamond shape of disappointment out of my father's heart.

I had no choice, anyway. People hand-over-handed me down to the plane from the grandstand.

The *Gypsy Moth* was a two-seater Curtiss Jenny. The pilot lifted me into the backseat.

"Hi, I'm Ike!" he said. "What's your name, son?"

I let out the air that I had crammed inside my lungs. "Reuben," I answered.

Ike encased my head in a leather helmet with goggles made for a giant. "Reuben, you're no bigger than a peanut. What do they call you at school?"

"Shrimp-boats," I answered miserably.

"Listen here, Reuben. They'll never call you Shrimp-boats again. After this you'll be a medal-of-honor hero in this corn-fed town! Okay?"

"Yes, sir."

"Ain't scared, now?"

"No, sir."

"Roger. Now listen good. This here plane has no brakes, so we'll have a bumpy landing. Boys love it. We'll do three barrel rolls . . . that's turning the plane upside down midair, but you're strapped in, so it don't matter. Then a couple of Immelman turns, and the grand finale is a wingover. That's where you fly straight up for a thousand feet, then nose-dive straight down a thousand. It don't take but twenty seconds, but it's guaranteed to give the crowd heart failure. Don't fret about

the harness busting. The last man who wore 'em was the fat man at the circus."

The earth left us. My heart went faster than the propellers of the *Gypsy Moth*. I did not breathe at all. And so behind my eyes my mind turned snow white, through the barrel rolls, and the Immelman, and the dive.

The names of things dropped away from me. I don't remember spinning, landing, or what anyone said except for Mary Ellen.

"You're sicker than a pig and greener than a dollar bill," said Mary Ellen. "I'm not sitting next to you in the car home."

My mother gave me sassafras tea to slow down my pulse.

She looked needles at my father more than once because she did not hold with airplaning.

But the day lingered around Father like a sun-warm halo. He called me "My Air Ace," not knowing my heart had stopped beating after the first barrel roll in the *Gypsy Moth*; not knowing Ike had jump-started me back to life by thumping me on the chest and giving me a shot of raw fire from his pocket flask.

"You can do anything in the whole wide world after that!" said Father when he kissed me good night.

I didn't tell him the truth. Something was wrong with me, clear as day. "Boys love it," Ike had said. I didn't. Mary Ellen was right. I was a born yellow coward. I swore to God I would never go higher than our attic window for as long as I lived if only He would keep me away from airplanes.

CHAPTER TWO

DREAMS

"YOUR FATHER has dreams on the side, Reuben," my mother told me. She and I were planting nasturtiums in the center of a truck tire painted white. "In his dreams he is Charles Lindbergh flying the Atlantic Ocean. Who can explain dreams?"

In the real world my father was a dancing teacher, two flights upstairs in the Hubbard Building on Ivory Street.

Father always kept a colored silk handkerchief in his breast pocket. "Just like the President of the United States," he said.

Ladies of the town learned ballroom dancing from my father. They fox-trotted after him, circling the waxed floors of the Hubbard Building, humming "Good Night Irene."

"Not a one of them can hold a candle to your mother," Father said.

My mother was the cook at the Lariat Café. Her customers were truck drivers who stopped for her chicken à la king and deep-dish apple pie in the middle of their long roads east or west.

"My boys are good boys," said my mother about the truck drivers. "But there isn't a one of them who's a patch on your father."

We had everything a person could need, my

mother said. Our nasturtiums bloomed in their white tire bed, under the clearest blue summer skies and sun.

Saturday mornings Walter Olshan drove up in a Pontiac truck, his sheepdog, Binney, sitting in the front seat. We bought sausages from Mr. Olshan. To me he looked exactly like one of his Poland China hogs in overalls.

After church on Sundays my father made griddle cakes and pepper pork sausage for Sunday breakfast. "We live like kings," said my father.

When the Beale Brothers' circus came to Ambler, I won a Silver Dollar Indian knife at the pitch-penny. It was the most beautiful thing I had ever owned. That time was like warm air safely cupped in my hands.

*   *   *

Suddenly out of nowhere the dust storms came up.

Dust blew through the closed windows of all the houses. It blew into the ears of dogs and the farmers' trouser cuffs. Little by little our green prairies turned the color of meal crackers. Dust devils blew around your ankles peevishly for no reason in the world.

Mothers complained that nothing could be kept clean for more than a minute. The corn shriveled in the fields.

No one wanted to learn to dance that year. Not many people came to eat at the Lariat Café. First my father lost his job. Then my mother lost hers.

The dust blew away people's work and all their life savings. The bank took away the Olshans' farm. The Olshans left town. Mr.

Olshan hardly said good-bye, as if he'd done something wrong and was ashamed.

Binney would not go with them. She walked the rounds of families that made up Mr. Olshan's Saturday trips to town. I found her outside our front gate. Her coat was as tangled as a tumbleweed. She drank a quart bowl of water and then another.

"We can hardly feed ourselves, much less a dog," my mother said. "But all the same we can't fail to take her in."

Binney agreed to sleep on my bed. She put her head on my shoulder and sighed the sigh of a person who's afraid to cry in front of other people.

My father found a two-week job as night watchman at a drilling station for five dollars a week.

At six o'clock my mother and I brought his supper out to him on the bus.

While we waited at the bus stop, people we didn't even know told us where they were going.

"We're heading for California!" they shouted, just as though they were heading for heaven.

"They're going nowhere in a hurry," whispered my mother.

But the word *California* put a jump in my heart. The letters of the word were made of blue water and lemon trees. Oklahoma was weed brown.

One night there was a prairie fire south of town. My mother and I saw it licking up against the brown sky. We could hear it taking up power.

At three minutes to ten one of the far-away oil wells caught fire. It exploded in flames like a shower of bombs I had seen in the newsreels.

"Which drilling station? Which one?" my mother asked. There were six oil drilling rigs you could see from the attic window. We couldn't tell them apart.

We did not know whether my father was at this moment not only dead, but gone entirely from the face of the earth, even his watch and shoes.

If the fire was at a different well, Father might be safe. But then, someone else's father had caught fire. We did not want to hope for this out loud and so we said nothing. My mother rubbed cocoa butter into her hands.

"Go to bed, Reuben," my mother told me. "Go to bed."

I told myself if I went to sleep my father would surely be dead. I made myself drink coffee with sugar and I stayed awake with my mother. There were no telephones in Ambler at that time. We had only the *tick-tick* of the kitchen clock before his bus came and we would hear or not hear him open the door.

"Until he comes we will be in the tunnel of fear," said my mother, "and we will see no end to it."

At last my mother's head dropped in sleep.

I crept upstairs and got out my precious Silver Dollar knife. Then I raced down the stairs, out the door, and across town to the First Presbyterian Church.

"Please, God, I will give you my most

precious gift. Please make it not Father's oil well," I said.

Then I dropped the knife in the mail slot for God to pick up.

But whatever had happened was forever sealed away. I knew even God had no power to swing low and undo what was done.

I fell asleep on Binney's furry side beside the door. I dreamed my father had turned into a pillar of fire.

At sunrise Father's hand turned the doorknob, and the tunnel of fear became a field of light.

I told him about my Indian knife in the mail slot of the church.

"Could it be that I sucked you back from God?" I asked.

"If such a thing could happen," said Father,

"to be sucked back through fire and time itself, I do believe I would have the memory of it."

"But it could happen!" I wanted it to have happened.

"It was not my time to go," said Father.

CHAPTER THREE

DUST

ONE MONDAY morning the windows of the Lariat Café were boarded up like blindfolded eyes. The Hubbard Building was locked and still.

Father said he was sure some work was bound to come along. "Reuben," my mother and father told me, "without you to love we would have nothing."

Every day they looked at the help-wanted ads in the newspapers, but no one had any work to offer.

One evening my father brought home a half-dozen eggs folded up in a newspaper hat. Mother took the eggs and made us an omelette for supper. Father uncrumpled the paper hat and spread it out on the kitchen table.

"This is a newspaper all the way from Minnesota!" said my father.

"What's going on up there in Minnesota?" asked my mother.

"Listen to this!" said my father.

WANTED

FOR IMMEDIATE EMPLOYMENT

WINGWALKER

MUST BE BRAVE

AND LIGHT ON THE FEET

WRITE TO

DIXIE BELLE

P.O. BOX 45

ST. PAUL, MINNESOTA

"Don't be silly, Howard," my mother said.

But my father wrote to Dixie Belle with-out telling my mother. I know because I posted the letter for him. The next week an answer came.

June 15, 1934

Dear Howard,

I was about to give up on finding anyone. I am delighted you will take the job. A dancing teacher is just the right fellow for this line of work. Salary is $20 an hour. By the way, it's not as dangerous up on the wing as most people imagine. Meet me at the corner of Malamute and Main, downtown St. Paul, at noon on the Fourth of July.

Yours truly,

Dixie Belle

"Howard, you can't become a wing-walker," said my mother.

"I can and I will," said my father.

All evening my mother said no. My father said yes. My father said twenty dollars an hour would pay all the bills for the next five years. My mother said there wouldn't be anything but one big hospital bill for the next five years.

I fell asleep while they argued. When I woke the argument had been settled. They had flipped a coin, and my father had won.

The next day they sold all our furniture and bought a brand-new Studebaker. Binney stayed with Mary Ellen and my aunt Carmen Hockerbee, who said a dog was the next-best thing to having a man around the house.

CHAPTER FOUR

WIDE WORLD

WE LEFT OKLAHOMA on June 29, 1934, at six in the morning, taking Route 480 north as far as the Missouri line.

Each day we drove as far as we could, eating hot dogs in peculiar restaurants, filling up with strange kinds of gas.

Every night villages of cabins appeared in the ground mist just in time for us to go to bed. The cabins were built in clearings on the hillsides. Each set had differently colored shutters. Some had names like Larkspur or

Bluebird that made my mother happy. The cabins came up out of the soft falling blueness of night, and disappeared behind us as suddenly as the coming and going of the strange radio stations.

After five days we pulled out of Iowa and into Minnesota. "Land of a Thousand Lakes," said my mother, and I looked out the window, thinking I might see at least a hundred at one time.

Dixie was as good as her word. At exactly noon on the Fourth of July she met us at the corner of Malamute and Main in downtown St. Paul, Minnesota. Dixie's hair was cut short like a man's. She wore riding pants and lace-up boots. She wasted no time and led us, on her motorcycle, out of the city and into the green, dustless hills.

"Can you cook for a lot of people?" Dixie asked my mother.

"You bet I can," she answered.

"Good," said Dixie. "There's money to be made at the county fair canteen. Our regular cook just upped and left for New York City, so the job is yours if you want it."

My mother settled right in. She made breakfast and supper for the performers who followed the fair from county to county. For the first time since the Lariat Café closed, she was able to make chicken à la king and deep-dish apple pie. "My signature dishes," said my mother.

Dixie introduced us to the Fat Man, the Tattooed Lady, the Fire Eater, and the Human Snake.

There wasn't a living soul in Ambler

black like the Fat Man. No one who had tattoos. Nobody who'd dare eat fire or climb
into a glass bottle.

The first night at the fair I shivered,
wrapped in cotton blankets, sure that one of
them would come in and watch me sleeping.

Father poked his head under my tent door.

"Will you fall off the wing, Father?" I
asked.

"Do I fall on the dance floor?" he asked,
winking at me.

"But it's different."

"The wing has gravel bits varnished on
the surface. I can wear a harness if I like, and
I put rubber taps on my shoes. So long as you
don't try foolishness, like jumping onto the
wing of another plane midair, it's perfectly
safe," he said.

*What will happen if you fall into the clouds?
What will happen to Mother and to me?* I asked him
with my eyes.

The next morning Dixie showed my
father how to go up on the wing. Her airplane was called *The Land of Cotton*, painted
in big letters on both sides. My mother
wouldn't watch, but I did. Away they flew
in the cockpit together, leaving the earth
and me behind. He didn't come out on the
wing until Dixie made slow circles above the
fairgrounds. Father looked the way he
always did when he turned on the Victrola
to show the first three or four steps of the
fox-trot.

"Is that your pa?" asked a voice to my side.

It was the Fat Man. "Brave pa you've
got, boy," he said. "My name's Otto."

I shook Otto's enormous hand, as big as a grizzly bear's paw.

"Son," said Otto, "You're shaking like a preacher at a tent revival."

"I'm scared to lose my pa," I said.

"God don't push no papas off the wings of airplanes," said Otto. "They all come down, unless they're hotheads."

"My pa's not a hothead," I said.

"Then he'll come down safe as a pie. How would you like to learn a trick or two?" Otto asked.

"Yes," I said. I looked up into Otto's tiger-colored eyes. If I learned to do a magic trick, Father might come down safely.

Otto asked where I was from.

"Ambler, Oklahoma," I answered.

"Hog-farm country," said Otto.

"Yes, sir."

Otto smiled. One of his main front teeth was entirely gold.

He asked me if I'd ever seen a colored man before.

"Only in magazines," I answered.

"Every living soul in Ambler is as pink as a shoat?" Otto asked.

"Yes, sir," I answered.

"Boy, you can call me Otto," said Otto.

Otto taught me how to use fanning powder to make playing cards fly in and out of your hands like birds. Then he taught me how to triple cut and shuffle, and the hidden-queen trick.

I tried, and the cards spurted across the grass.

Otto was as patient as an old mother

bird. He told me he wore a size 100 suit, made specially in the city of New Orleans. He taught me how to walk a quarter back and forth across the tops of my fingers.

"Still scared?" Otto asked.

I didn't want to look up in the sky.

"Here," said Otto. "If you can find the queen of spades facedown, I guarantee he'll be fine."

Otto fanned out the deck of cards. At random I pulled the queen correctly from the middle, and Father came down safely from the sky.

"How did you know which card I would pick?" I asked Otto.

But Otto just showed me his twenty-four-carat-gold front tooth.

* * *

The first day of the fair was outside Lucky City. Glossy oxen and chickens as deluxe as Sunday hats were brought to the fairground.

My new friend Otto took me all around. At two in the afternoon we watched Dixie take off in *The Land of Cotton* with my father in the cockpit. Dixie circled the grounds, and my father went out on the wing. He stood tall and waved to the crowds. "What a man!" said Otto.

I held my breath. My eye was on Father's feet dancing like a bee's. I held my breath, and *The Land of Cotton* landed soft as a dove.

At dinner our second night I sat next to the Tattooed Lady. She told us her name was Josephine.

Josephine could see I didn't like her tattoos. Everybody in Ambler would have said a person belonged smack in the loony bin who had gone and had herself tattooed like that. The loony bin was far away in the state capital, but I was scared to death of anybody who might belong in it.

"You are just as polite as a potato chip," she said, "but I bet you want to ask me why I have all these tattoos."

I nodded my head.

"I was born with red and purple marks all over me. The children at school called me names. No one wanted to look at me. I was not happy. When I grew up I asked a great artist to cover me with beautiful pictures of birds and flowers. Then I joined the fair and now people drive miles to see me. I have my

own tent, enough to eat, good friends, and I am happy.

"This was the best apple Betty I have ever eaten," Josephine said to my mother. "If you entered it in the baking contest tomorrow it would win a prize."

My mother was so happy that all the tired lines around her eyes left, and she smiled like a movie star.

Josephine invited me into her tent to see a black top hat in a box. "It once belonged to Abraham Lincoln," she said. "His name's signed in the crown."

I held the hat. "You can try it on any old time you want to come in," said Josephine.

*   *   *

After three days the fair moved to the next county and started up all over again with new prize hogs and prize roosters. I saw the world's largest duck egg come in on the back seat of a Packard.

This time when my father went up, he did a samba step on the wing. He always wore his best black suit with the silk handkerchief and kept his shoes carefully shined. My mother still wouldn't watch him, but I never missed a turn. I could make the quarter fall unseen between my fingers and down into the cuff of my shirtsleeve, just like Otto.

On the side of a barn, back home in Ambler, was a big painted advertisement for Goblin Chewing Tobacco.

Here at the fair, Buck, the Fire Eater, looked just exactly like the devil on the can.

I didn't go near the Fire Eater for just this reason.

One afternoon I went into our caravan for a cookie and there he was, mouth open and crying . . . a grown man!

My mother saw me. "Go get some ice at the lunch tent, Reuben," she said. "Quick! Buck here had an accident this morning."

I ran. I came back with ice and purple gentian ointment that I got from the stable first-aid kit. Buck had no money for a doctor.

My mother tended him all afternoon. By evening Buck was able to drink a glass of cream soda.

"Thank you, ma'am," said Buck. He winked at me. "Gonna teach you to juggle, Reuben," he said. "Start with three balls."

"No throwing knives or eating fire," said my mother.

Buck told us he was a farmer's son from Slapper, Texas. He had picked so much cotton in his young life that he grew up almost field blind.

One day three jugglers blew into town. When they had finished performing on the hood of their Model A, they got to talking about bright lights and music in the city of Galveston. On the Galveston docks the sailors stepped off boats from every country in the world and danced all night.

"I began to cry like a baby when I heard of this," said Buck. "I knew I would never get out of Slapper if I didn't take a chance, so I left my mama and my papa without even a good-bye. I stealed away in the back of the jugglers' car,

and they didn't find me until it was too late. They learned me how to juggle and I got good. Then I started with swords and torches."

"Did you ever write home and tell your folks you are still in the land of the living?" asked my mother.

"No, ma'am. I never did know how to write."

"Can they read if they get a letter from you?" asked my mother.

"They can get the preacher to read it for 'em," said Buck.

I wrote down a whole letter for Buck. He touched every word with his forefinger before we put it in an envelope.

"Now your mother and father won't be lost to you at all," I said to Buck, "and they won't have lost you either."

We walked out to the highway to mail Buck's letter.

"I never met up with no boy like you," said Buck. "So young and all and can read and write good as a schoolteacher. Where you come from? The movies?"

"I lived in a little town where nothing happened," I said. "Nobody but plain white farm people living slow. Every day they say the same thing. Every week they wear the same good pair of shoes to church. I used to count Sunday shoes under the pews. Then the dust came and we had to leave."

"You must be scared of us, me and Dingo and Tattooed Josie."

"I'm more scared of my cousin Mary Ellen Hockerbee," I said.

* * *

After three days the fair moved to the next county. In the new fairgrounds were thirty Percheron draft horses, all entered in a pulling contest. Champion fiddlers played off and champion clog dancers danced off against one another all night long on the stage inside the main tent.

Deep in my bed I listened to the fiddlers' sweet homesick music from across the field. The clog dancers' feet pounded faster than galloping horse hooves. I had watched them so many times I could follow them with my mind's eye. On the main stage, bright teeth and eyes gleamed sweaty orange under the battery lamps in the heavy heat of the tent.

Blinky with sleep, I breathed the smells of the earth and fresh-cut hay stubble, trampled

cigars, and cotton candy that wandered up through a hole in the floor of my tent.

As I fell into dreams, the fiddlers' tent whirled on to a secret midnight among the stars that I never seemed able to stay awake to see.

My father snored. My mother stayed up knitting in the dark, her needles clicking like crickets.

* * *

We went from county to county across Minnesota, Wisconsin, Illinois, Indiana, and into Ohio. Each time my father added a new dance step—rumba, fox-trot, two-step—to his wing-walk. My mother never watched my father on the wing of Dixie's plane. I never missed it.

"I'd like to take Reuben up on the wing

before the summer's over," my father said.

"Over my dead body," my mother answered.

"He'll be perfectly safe," said my father.

My mother gave my father a needle look with her eyes that would have curdled a glass of milk. "Reuben's got more sense than to go onto the wing of a plane," Mama said.

Girly-pants mama's boy. I'm gonna tell! sang an invisible Mary Ellen.

* * *

In late August of that year we went all the way to Bell County, Kentucky. The wind was a little chill in the evening. The chatter of the grown-ups turned to what would become of us when the cold came. I wanted to go home. But I guessed there was no Ambler to go back to.

"By this time the dust has gone through the windows of my bedroom like drifts of snow," said my mother so sadly. "Losing home is like losing your shadow. You walk on by, and no one knows that you have been there."

Suddenly I knew there was no more Mary Ellen and no third-grade class for her to tell about me and make them laugh. I was on my own.

I was on my way to Otto's caravan to play Go Fish with Josephine and Buck when I heard a voice behind me.

"Boy, how would you like to get into a bottle?" It was the Human Snake. I forgot all about the Go Fish game.

The Human Snake's name was Frank Dingo. He said if he could get his head through an opening, the rest of his body just followed. His most famous trick was to get into an army surplus twenty-gallon corn-oil bottle. I tried all evening, but I didn't get the hang of it.

When it was bedtime, Frank Dingo said, "It's just a stunt to get into a bottle. That's all it is. But your pa . . . a man who can dance on the wing of a plane is the man of the hour. He's most likely teaching you how to do it."

"I got so scared of an airplane once, I promised God I'd never go higher than the attic window," I said.

"Hold your father's hand," said Frank Dingo.

*   *   *

September crept up on August. The last fair of the summer was in Monroe County.

Dixie had *The Land of Cotton* fitted out with new tires and a new coat of silver paint for the grand finale. My father and I inspected the undercarriage for nicks and scratches.

"Ready, Howard?" Dixie asked from the cockpit.

"Stone pitting on the belly, Dixie," my father answered. "Hold on, and we'll shine her up.

"Fall is coming, then winter," said my father as we polished the panels of *The Land of Cotton*.

"What will we do?" I asked.

"We never know what's around the next bend in the river, do we?" said my father. "Meantime, how would you like to go out on the wing with me?"

"Ready, Howard?" Dixie called.

"It's now or never, Reuben," said my father.

I saw pride sparkling in my father's eyes like stars.

The Land of Cotton was a two-seater Swallow. I had to squeeze into my father's lap on the way up.

The plane steadied and slowed. Father grabbed the struts and swung himself out onto the wing. He held his hand out to me. We stood on the wing together. I didn't feel much worse than standing in a prairie squall.

My father did a tango step and waved to the crowds. Far below us my four friends, Otto, Josephine, Buck, and Frank Dingo, waved in a sea of a thousand people.

Then he pointed to the Great Smoky

Mountains off in the southeast, and the Cumberland River that elbowed its way, sparkly as a necklace, down through Tennessee. The clean sunny air rushed over and around us as if we were birds.